INSECT
METAMORPHOSIS
FROM EGG TO ADULT

Ron and Nancy Goor

ATHENEUM   **NEW YORK**

With love, to Alex and Dan

Atheneum
Macmillan Publishing Company
866 Third Avenue
New York, New York 10022
Collier Macmillan Canada, Inc.

Printed and bound in China

10   9   8   7   6   5   4

Library of Congress Cataloging-in-Publication Data
Goor, Ron.
Insect metamorphosis / by Ron and Nancy Goor.—1st ed.
p.   cm.   Bibliography: p.   Includes index.
Summary: Explains how insects grow, describing the various stages
of incomplete and complete metamorphosis.
ISBN 0-689-31445-0
1. Insects—Metamorphosis—Juvenile literature.   [1. Insects—
Metamorphosis.]   I. Goor, Nancy.   II. Title.
QL494.5.G66   1990   595.7'031—dc20   89-15144   CIP   AC

Monarch egg photo (p. 2) by Selwyn Sacks
Cecropia moth cocoon photo (p. 14) by Mr. Lynn M. Stone/ BRUCE COLMAN INC., New York

The photo on the title page is of a silver spotted skipper butterfly.

Contents

Large milkweed bugs, adults and nymphs

Eastern tiger swallowtail caterpillar

nsects have special ways of growing. They grow in stages, not continuously as we do. Some insects look totally different at each stage, other insects look like little adults at each stage. These two special ways of growing in stages are called *complete metamorphosis* and *incomplete metamorphosis.*

Eastern tiger swallowtail butterfly

COMPLETE METAMORPHOSIS

Monarch butterflies, like many other insects, go through four different stages to become adults. They look totally different at each stage. These are the four stages:

Egg

Larva

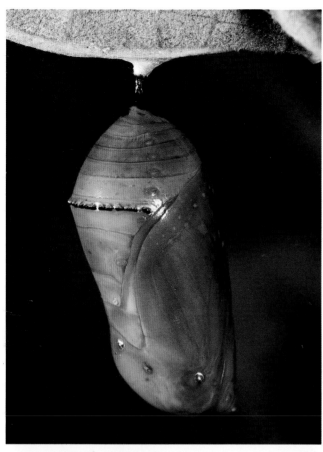

Pupa Look closely to see the butterfly inside.

Adult

This way of growing is called complete metamorphosis.

HICKORY HORNED DEVIL CATERPILLARS

The egg is the first stage of an insect's life.

Adult female insects lay eggs where they will not be seen—on the underside of a leaf, on the bark of a tree, on water, sometimes even inside other insects.

Most eggs hatch in the spring or summer, when it is warm. Then there is lots of food for the young insects to eat. These eggs were laid under a leaf. They are hidden so they will not be found and eaten.

Look closely. You can see a black caterpillar curled up inside each egg.

To hatch, a caterpillar eats a hole in its egg case and crawls out. After hatching, caterpillars nibble on their egg cases for extra energy.

4

A caterpillar is a *larva*. The larva is the second stage in an insect's life. This caterpillar is called a hickory horned devil.

At first, the caterpillar's skin is soft and wet. After the skin dries, the caterpillar looks different. The eight horns folded behind its head straighten out. They are long and spiked. They make the caterpillar look scary even though it is harmless.

The caterpillar is very tiny. It is ready to begin the important job of eating. Eating is serious business for all insects. The hickory horned devil will eat enough leaves to grow from one-quarter inch long to seven inches in just two months.

The caterpillar eats and grows. But, it does not grow like we do. Its skeleton is on the outside—where humans have skin. This outside skeleton is called an *exoskeleton*. It is hard like a suit of armor.

The exoskeleton protects the insect. It gives it shape and keeps it from drying out. But, like a suit of armor, the exoskeleton cannot grow. It cannot stretch. To grow larger, the caterpillar must break out of its exoskeleton. This is called *molting*.

When an insect is ready to molt, its exoskeleton splits down the back and the insect pulls itself out. This is hard work. Imagine how difficult it would be to wriggle out of a skintight bag without using your hands. Molting is dangerous, for a molting caterpillar is helpless. If a bird attacks it, the caterpillar cannot move away. If the caterpillar is unable to wriggle out of its skin, it will die.

This molting caterpillar is in trouble. Part of its new exoskeleton is stuck to its old exoskeleton. If the insect tears a hole in the new exoskeleton, it will bleed to death. The caterpillar arches its body and tugs. The new piece of skin pulls away. The caterpillar is safe.

Black hickory horned devil shortly after hatching

Brown hickory horned devil after molting

Tan hickory horned devil after molting

Folded up underneath the old exoskeleton is a new larger one. The newly molted caterpillar puffs its new exoskeleton full of air. Soon the exoskeleton hardens and the caterpillar returns to eating. It continues to eat until it has replaced all the air with food. It will molt many times. Each time it becomes larger and changes color. The hickory horned devil changes from black to brown to tan to green.

Green hickory horned devil after molting

In the fall, when the hickory horned devil is fully grown, it stops eating. Some time in the middle of September, it crawls down from the top branches of a walnut, sweet gum, or hickory tree and wanders along the ground until it finds a place to burrow. It digs four to six inches into the earth and hollows out a chamber.

The caterpillar lies very still in its chamber. During the next few days, it loses water from its body and shrinks to about one-third its full-grown size.

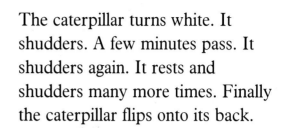

The caterpillar turns white. It shudders. A few minutes pass. It shudders again. It rests and shudders many more times. Finally the caterpillar flips onto its back.

The exoskeleton at the back of its head splits open. The caterpillar thrashes back and forth to wriggle out of its exoskeleton.

It is now a *pupa*. The pupa is the third stage of an insect's life.

Many changes are taking place inside the pupa. It is becoming an adult moth. Look closely. Can you see the wings and antennae of the adult moth?

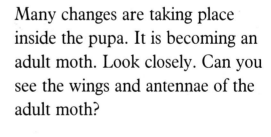

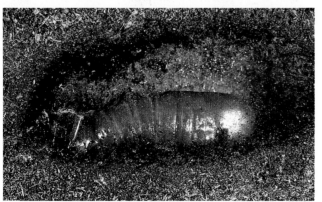

When the pupal skin dries, it turns a rich brown. The hickory horned devil pupa spends the fall, winter, and spring in its underground chamber, tucked away from enemies and the cold weather.

In the summer, when the earth warms, the pupa stirs. The skin behind its head splits and the adult climbs out. It digs itself out of the ground and climbs onto a twig or leaf. It is no longer an egg. It is no longer a big, green caterpillar. It is no longer a pupa. It has become an adult. It has become a magnificent royal walnut moth.

The moth's wings are folded and wet. It pumps blood into them and they stiffen. When they are dry, the moth will be able to fly.

The adult moth has no mouth parts. It cannot eat. It lives just long enough to find a mate. Female moths give off a special odor to attract males. This odor is called a *pheromone*. Male moths use chemical sensors on their large, feathery antennae to "smell" a female moth's pheromones. A male moth can follow the odor from as far as two miles away. When he reaches the female, they mate.

After mating, the female royal walnut moth lays eggs on a leaf. Soon the eggs will hatch and the life story of the hickory horned devil will begin again.

MOURNING CLOAK BUTTERFLIES

The mourning cloak caterpillar also hatches out of an egg. It eats and eats. It molts many times.

In the last days of summer, the mourning cloak caterpillar attaches itself to a twig by a stalk of silk and hangs upside down. It wriggles out of its skin. The caterpillar has become a pupa. The pupa of a butterfly is called a *chrysalis*. Because the mourning cloak chrysalis looks like a dead leaf, other animals leave it alone. Many changes are taking place inside the chrysalis.

In early spring, the adult insect comes out of the chrysalis. It is now a beautiful brown mourning cloak butterfly.

Wings closed   Wings opened

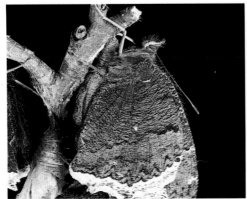

13

CECROPIA MOTHS

The cecropia moth caterpillar hatches out of an egg. It eats and grows and molts all summer until it is a big, green caterpillar almost four and one-half inches long. At the summer's end, it becomes a pupa in a *cocoon* it spins of its own silk, and it spends the fall and winter well hidden among branches and leaves. In the spring, the cecropia moth emerges from its tough, gray cocoon. With a wingspan of more than six inches, the cecropia moth is the largest moth in North America.

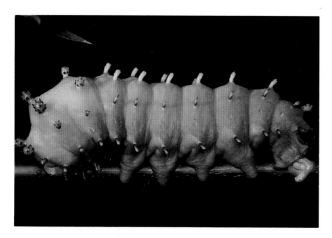

MOSQUITOES

Mosquitoes also have four stages in their life story.

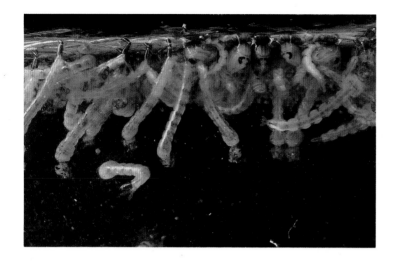

Mosquitoes lay their eggs on water—in ponds, in marshes, even in puddles in discarded tires. The larvae hatch out in the water. Mosquito larvae are called wrigglers. They wriggle to the bottom to eat. They wriggle to the surface to breathe. Wrigglers breathe through tubes in their rear ends.

Floating beneath the wrigglers is a mosquito pupa. It looks like a comma. The pupae of most insects stay very still, but mosquito pupae move through the water.

Many changes are taking place inside the pupa. The pupa is changing into an adult mosquito. In two or three days, the adult mosquito will pull itself out of the pupal case on the surface of the water.

Adult male

You can tell if a mosquito is male by looking at its antennae. Male mosquitoes have feathery antennae. They use their feathery antennae to hear. They find mates by listening for the buzz female mosquitoes make beating their wings.

Only the female mosquito bites. She must have a meal of blood before she can produce eggs. She bites an animal—perhaps you—to get that meal.

PAPER WASPS

Paper wasps are social insects like bees, ants, and termites. They live together in nests. You can see all four life stages of the paper wasp in this picture. Small white eggs occupy almost all the top cells of the nest. Several larvae fill cells on the right in the second row. Adults feed them with a paste of chewed up insects. Each cell that is covered with a cap of silk contains a pupa. The pupae do not eat. They are making the tremendous change from pupa to adult. When the change is complete, the adult wasp bites its way out of the cell.

BRACONID WASPS

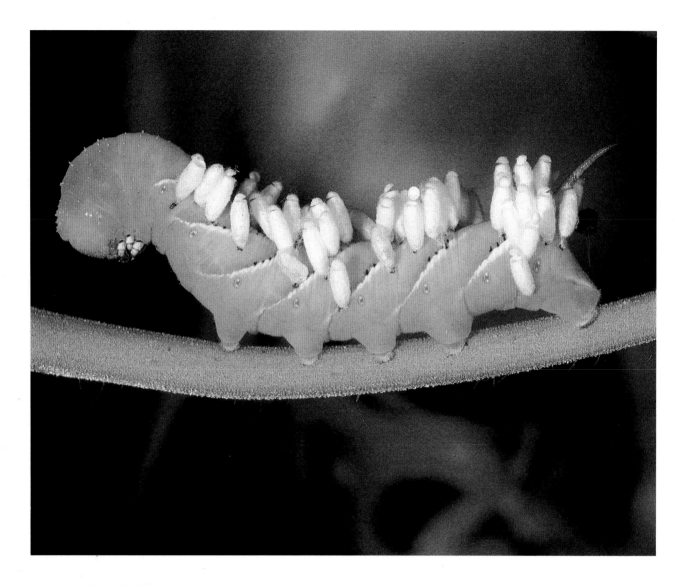

Female braconid wasps lay their eggs inside living tomato hornworm caterpillars. The wasp larvae hatch inside the caterpillars. They eat up the caterpillars' insides.

One morning, the caterpillar looks perfectly normal. That night, tiny white balloons appear all over the caterpillar's body. These balloons are cocoons. Inside are the wasp pupae. When the pupae become adults, the tops of the cocoons pop open and the wasps fly out. The caterpillar, now an empty shell, soon dies.

Wasps, butterflies, moths, beetles, bees, ants, and flies—these are some of the many insects that change from egg to larva to pupa to adult.

Ladybird beetle larva eating aphids

Ladybird beetle

Polyphemus moth caterpillar

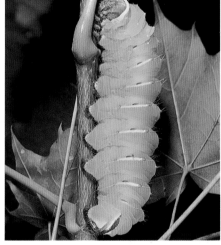

Polyphemus moth

Milkweed leaf beetle eggs

Milkweed leaf beetle

INCOMPLETE METAMORPHOSIS

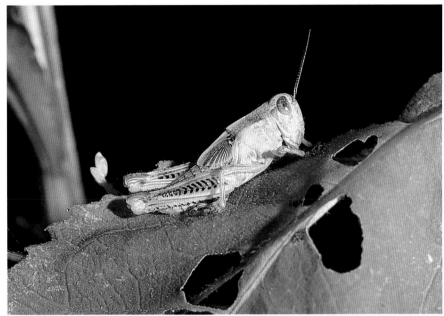

Nymph

Adult

Other insects, such as grasshoppers (shown here), praying mantids, and true bugs, do not change as they grow. They begin as eggs, but they do not hatch into larvae. When they hatch, they look just like adult insects, only smaller. These newly hatched insects are called *nymphs*.

Dead leaf mantid nymph

Dead leaf mantid adult

Boxelder bug nymph

Boxelder bug adult

Nymphs have small wing buds instead of wings. They cannot fly. They molt many times, but they do not become pupae. Each time they molt, they become larger. When they pull themselves out of their exoskeleton for the last molt, they have wings and they can mate. They have become adults. This change from egg to nymph to adult is called incomplete metamorphosis.

PRAYING MANTIDS

Adult female mantids make a foamy liquid in which to lay their eggs. The egg cases harden on twigs and protect the eggs from hungry enemies and the cold winter.

In the spring, praying mantid nymphs hatch from their egg cases. They look just like tiny adult mantids without wings. Because they are so small, these mantids can only catch tiny insects. Some mantids eat each other. Only a few will survive. Praying mantids eat and molt until they are quite large. When they molt for the last time, they may be as large as five inches long. Adult mantids eat all sorts of insects. Some have been known to eat small snakes and hummingbirds.

Nymphs crawling away from egg case

Adult praying mantid

DRAGONFLIES

Dragonflies lay their eggs on plants near ponds or quiet streams. The dragonfly nymphs hatch out and live in the water. They have gills so they can breathe underwater. There, they molt many times.

The dragonfly nymph has a special lower lip for catching food. It is shaped like an arm with hooks. The nymph quietly waits for a tadpole, insect, or even a small fish to swim close. In a flash, the nymph shoots out its lip and grabs its dinner.

When the dragonfly nymph is ready to molt for the last time, it climbs out of the water onto a reed. The nymph's exoskeleton splits behind the head and down its back and the adult dragonfly pulls itself out.

Dragonfly nymph

Exoskeleton of dragonfly nymph

Dragonfly adult

The adult dragonfly must first dry its wings before it can fly. Dragonflies are the best flyers of all insects. Some can fly as fast as sixty miles per hour.

CICADAS

Adult female cicadas lay their eggs in slits they make in branches of trees. When the nymphs hatch out they drop to the ground and burrow into the earth. They live underground for many years. To eat, they suck sap from tree roots. In the spring of their seventeenth year, they dig out of the ground. They climb up trees and telephone poles to make their final molt.

Cicada nymph climbing up telephone pole

Adult cicada emerging from nymph case

The exoskeleton behind the cicada's head splits open and the cicada pulls itself out, leaving behind its empty exoskeleton. You have probably seen many of these exoskeletons attached to trees, poles, and buildings.

23

At first, the adult cicada is soft and white. Soon its new exoskeleton dries and becomes hard and dark. Its wings become stiff and it flies into the trees. Have you heard the loud, whirring sound that fills the air on hot summer days? To attract female cicadas, males sing a "love song" by vibrating muscles in their abdomens.

Every spring and summer, some cicadas end their long stay in the ground to become adults. But in 1987, an enormous brood of millions of cicadas hatched out. If you took a walk late at night, you would see hundreds of cicadas crawling across streets. They covered every upright surface—even blades of grass. Their mating song was deafening. Such a gigantic brood of cicadas will appear again in 2004.

Adult cicada and nymph case

Adult cicada

Giant waterbug carrying eggs on its back

An insect hatches out of an egg into a larva or a nymph. It eats and grows so it can become an adult. So it can mate. So more eggs can be laid. So there will be more insects to mate and lay more eggs.

INDEX